Guinevere Soussan

The Princess and the GIANt

FAIRY TALES

BEAN STALKS and other magic plants

BICYCLE REPAIR

BIG Book of BEDTIME TALES

How to TAME YOUR GIANT

For Suzi and George xx
C. H.

To Joanne, Roz, Nadine, Karen, and Bex—for all the love, laughs, and persistence!
S. W.

First U.S. edition 2015

Library of Congress Catalog Card Number 2014955414
ISBN 978-0-7636-8007-7

15 16 17 18 19 20 GBL 10 9 8 7 6 5 4 3 2 1

Printed in Shenzhen, Guangdong, China

This book was typeset in ThrohandInk.
The illustrations were done in mixed media.

Nosy Crow
an imprint of
Candlewick Press
99 Dover Street
Somerville, Massachusetts 02144

www.nosycrow.com
www.candlewick.com

The Princess and the Giant

Caryl Hart

Sarah Warburton

nosy crow

An imprint of Candlewick Press

A little princess lived inside
a little tiny house.
Her servant was a tabby cat.
Her butler was a mouse.

Her father made the porridge,
and her mother chopped the wood,
while Princess Sophie rode her bike,
as every princess should.

In the yard, behind the shed,
a magic bean stalk grew.
A giant lived right at the top
(as giants often do).

At night, the giant's stomping
made the people sob and shake.
"That selfish giant!" Sophie cried.
"He's keeping me awake!"

The princess asked her parents,
"Why are giants mean and bad?"
"Always have been," said her mother.
"Always will be," said her dad.

He found the book of fairy tales
they kept high on a shelf.
"It says so here, in black and white.
Look, read it for yourself."

So Sophie read a story set
in murky days of old,
when Jack climbed up a bean stalk
and discovered piles of gold.

A giant roared, "Get off my stuff!
I'll grind your bones for bread!
I'll FEE FI FO and FUM and then
I'll bop you on the head!"

STOMP!! STAMP!! SHAKE!!

That night poor Sophie tossed and turned.
"Our giant's such a pest.
If only he would go to sleep,
we might all get some rest!"

She read about a witch
who made a house from gingerbread.
It made her tummy rumble,
and a plan formed in her head.

Sophie pulled her jacket on
and laced her boots up tight.
She loaded up her backpack
then set out into the night.

She clambered up the bean stalk.
Brave Sophie didn't stop
till she reached the giant's castle,
which was balanced on the top.

Suddenly, the giant roared, "Who's creeping round outside?
A nasty little robber! Well, you'd better run and hide!"

OH NO, NOT YOU!

"I'm Sophie," said the princess.
She was quivering with fright.
"I've brought you a delicious snack
to help you sleep at night."

She'd cooked some lovely porridge
in her father's porridge pot.
"This should help you get to sleep.
It's creamy, sweet, and hot."

The giant growled, "This supper
wouldn't even feed a fly!"
But he ate the porridge anyway,
then slammed the door. "Good–bye!"

The giant's roars got louder. Sophie ran back home to bed.
She hugged her favorite teddy bear. "I'm glad you're here," she said.

All day long the giant howled. The people ran and hid.
But Sophie had another plan, so this is what she did. . . .

She read about a little girl who met three hungry bears.
And she wondered whether giants ever felt alone or scared.

She clambered up the bean stalk.
Brave Sophie didn't stop
till she reached the giant's castle,
which was balanced on the top.

STAMP!!

STOMP!!

SHAKE!!

The giant bellowed, "FEE FI FO! What IS that funny smell?
A horrid little girl has come to trick me. I can tell."
"It's only me," said Sophie as she held her backpack tight.
"I've brought some cuddly bears in case you're lonely in the night."

Then Sophie made some supper while the giant sulked and huffed.
"Giants don't need teddy bears! We're strong and brave and tough!"
But he gobbled up his porridge and he drank his milk and honey.
Then he took the biggest bear to bed and squeezed its furry tummy.

But still the giant couldn't sleep. The king cried, "Oh, my word!
He's making the most dreadful noise that I have ever heard."
Sophie hugged him tightly. "Daddy, don't be angry, please!
He might be like the princess whose bed was full of peas."

STOMP!!

STAMP!!

SHAKE!!

The king and queen were in despair, so Sophie filled a sack.
She dragged it to the garden, and she heaved it on her back.
She clambered up the bean stalk. Brave Sophie didn't stop
till she reached the giant's castle, which was balanced on the top.

The giant called, "FEE FI FO—OH!
It's you again, I see.
I suppose you'd better come inside
and have a cup of tea."

"I have the answer," Sophie cried.
"I know why you're so grumpy.
You can't get any sleep because
your bed's too hard and lumpy."

She pulled a mattress from the sack
and heaved it on the bed.
She gave the giant blankets
and a pillow for his head.

The giant ate his supper.
Then he gathered up his bears,
and he went to bed while Sophie
tiptoed down the castle stairs.

But . . .

the giant didn't sleep at all and soon was in a rage.

The queen cried, "Send the army NOW to lock him in a cage!"

Sophie looked up from her book. She'd tried her very best.

"There's nothing more that I can do," the princess said, "unless . . ."

Sophie grabbed her backpack, and she scrambled through the door.

"I can't imagine why I never thought of this before!"

She raced back up the bean stalk. Brave Sophie didn't stop

till she reached the giant's castle, which was balanced on the top.

"Stop that racket!" Sophie yelled.
"And get back into bed!"
The giant was so stunned and shocked,
he did as Sophie said.

The troops swarmed up the bean stalk. They were ready for a fight.
Then they heard a sweet and gentle voice that drifted through the night.

This HAS to work, thought Sophie
as she tucked his teddies in.
Then she pulled the softest blanket up
around the giant's chin.

"Are you feeling comfortable?" they heard the young voice say.
The soldiers stopped to listen, and they put their swords away.

Inside the castle, Sophie smiled.
"Oh, how could I forget?
You haven't had a story!
It's no wonder you're upset!"

She pulled the book out from her bag and read a bedtime story.
The giant AND the soldiers were soon fast asleep and snorey.

"I think I've done it!" Sophie cried.
"Our problems are no more.
The poor old giant couldn't sleep.
Now listen to him snore!"

"He's eaten up his supper, and he has some bears to hug.
I've read a lovely story—now he's happy, warm, and snug."

To celebrate the happy news, the king announced a feast.
They danced and partied all night long, till ten o'clock at least.
But as the people wandered home with party bags and cake,
there came a dreadful

THUD! THUD!!

THUD!

that made the whole world shake.

"The giant's coming!" screamed a boy.

"Quick! Everybody hide! He's going to make a giant pie and bake us all inside!"

"FEE FI FO!" the giant roared. The king and queen turned pale.

"Bring me Princess Sophie NOW. . . .

I want a fairy tale!"

The people stopped their panicking. They gasped in disbelief.
"Another story?" Sophie asked. "Well, THAT'S a big relief!
But why not read one by yourself?" she asked her giant friend.
"Just start at the beginning and keep going till the end."

"Oh, don't be silly, Sophie!" said the giant with a giggle.
"MY books aren't filled with stories; they're just full of tiny squiggles!"
"Those aren't squiggles," Sophie said. "They're words! We call it writing!
This writing tells us stories that are funny or exciting."

Sophie took the giant's hand. "I'll teach you how to read.
But first I need the army's help. There's something that I need."
She sent the giant home to bed, then rubbed her sleepy eyes.
"The next time that we meet"—she yawned—"you'll have a BIG surprise!"

The soldiers made a storybook.
The words were big and bold.
Inside they wrote the most
amazing stories ever told.

Once Upon
a time
there was
a magic
bean stalk.

Then Sophie taught her friend to read
by walking on the lines
And the giant read his giant book
one word at a time.

From that day forward, Sophie saw the giant every day.
Sometimes they took turns to read, and sometimes they'd just play.
The town was filled with joyful song and happy children's laughter . . .

and the princess and the giant both lived happy ever after.

THE END!